SICK F*CK

A Novella

Ash Ericmore

Written by: Ash Ericmore

Copyright © 2023 Ash Ericmore

All Rights Reserved. This is a work of fiction. No part of this publication may be reproduced, distributed, or transmitted in any form or by any means, except in the case of brief quotations embodied in critical reviews.

ISBN: 9798376425381

CHAPTER 1

Alex Cole was sitting in a rental Cherokee Jeep outside Newingland Primary School. There were some parents standing around the gates in the harsh autumnal winds, collars up, faces braced, waiting for the little munchkin release that occurred at two-thirty daily. Alex looked at the photo he'd busted out of the frame on top of the mantel piece of Jason Jones's living room.

Jason was his client.

Alex watched the commotion on the playground inside the fencing. A couple of teachers came out of the building followed by a line of brats. There was sudden screaming and waving as kids saw parents. You could see the looks in the parents eyes die, as they saw their freedom coming to an abrupt end. The teachers shouted, trying to keep the little fuckers in check. Alex looked for little Rush Jones. What kind of name was Rush Jones, anyway? He squinted over the heads of the parents to the line. Maybe he needed to get his eyes checked because it all looked like a fucking blur. Waiting until the commotion had reached the gates, Alex checked the mirrors before getting out the vehicle and crossing over. He had no desire to spend time with the doting dead-eyed families of these *children*. He stood at the back of the group. A couple of people gave him a glance, but looked away again without recognition. He guessed that newbies weren't found in the line very often.

That didn't make his life any easier.

Little bags of snot covered buggers were released

one at a time, and ragged looking parents suddenly switched persona to *Hey's* and *How was your day's*, before dragging the little ones off, not really listening to the answers.

As Alex got close to the gate, he made sure to familiarize himself with Rush—stood in the playground—and stuffed the picture back in his pocket. When he was stood facing the woman on the gate he smiled as warmly as he could. "Hi." he pushed his hands into his pocket, in anticipation of the first question. "My name's Logan Jones, I'm here to pick up my nephew, Rush."

The woman frowned and looked at her clipboard. All being well, he should have been added as a responsible person with the ability to pick up the little shit. He'd called ahead a couple of days ago pretending to be Jason Jones, and wanting to add his brother, Logan, who was visiting the family and *wouldn't it be nice if he could meet him from school, as a surprise?* They'd gone for it hook, line, and sinker, and hopefully, he would be allowed to take charge of the kid.

"Can I see some ID?" the woman asked.

Alex pulled a wallet from his pocket and opened it, pulling out the fake driver's license he'd knocked up in the office last week. The same one he'd used to rent the Cherokee. He handed it to the woman. It wasn't great, as far as fake ID's went, but this woman had probably never seen a fake in her life and wouldn't have a clue. Grabbing kids was surprisingly easy, even in this day and age.

She looked at it and passed it back, before waving

over Rush, who was looking at his feet in some dejected manner. "Rush, come here. Your uncle is here." Rush looked up and half walked, half ran over. He wasn't really old enough to be able to do either with skill yet. He looked like an uncoordinated baby deer, wearing an oversized puffer jacket with elastic coming out of each arm and a mitten attached, with a bobble hat on. He looked like a shit rip off of Home Alone's *Kevin*. He looked up at Alex and smiled, pushing out his fat little fucking cheeks.

He was six.

He should have been better at walking and shit by now, at least, that was what Alex thought, but what did he know? Alex crouched down to greet the rug rat. "Hey, Champ." He grinned at him and put his arms out and the retarded little fucker ran into them.

See? Stealing kids was really easy.

Alex stood, picking the kid up and nodded at the woman. "Thank you," he said, turning back to the Jeep. He checked both ways and then crossed over, fumbling about trying not to drop the fidgeting little fucker, while getting the back door open. He would have liked to just throw the squirmy little shit in the boot.

Maybe later.

He got the door open and then fought to get the kid into the car seat. He should have practised with it before he got there, but he was short of time what with renting the car and buying and fitting the car seat. He didn't think it was fitted right, but that really didn't matter. Not in the big scheme of things. He finally hooked the child in, and glanced over to the gates as he rounded the car. The woman stood there was watching him, looking more than a little concerned.

He waved over, pretending all was good.

He hopped in the car and started the engine.

"Where's Mummy?" The boy spoke for the first time.

Alex looked at him in the rear view mirror. Stupid kid was playing with his mittens like they were action figures or something. "She's waiting for you somewhere special," he said. "But it's a surprise."

"Yay," the kid screamed. Far too loudly for Alex's liking.

Alex took the car out into the traffic and away from the school. He had all the time in the world, but he wanted this over with quickly. He hated kids. *Really* fucking hated them. Which, in all fairness, meant that he liked his job, which was something.

CHAPTER 2

Alex pulled the car off the motorway into the industrial estate outside of the city. He had found the perfect place to do this over the last few days. He'd reconned the area looking for somewhere quiet, private, but close enough to the kid's school that he didn't have to put up with him in the car for too long.

Rush had behaved pretty well. He was quiet in the back seat, and entertained himself. If Alex had been someone else he might have felt sorry for the kid. But he wasn't. And he didn't.

He also didn't want to fuck him.

But he should.

The industrial estate was rundown. It was mostly shells of businesses and that meant it was perfect. He wasn't going to be there long, but it was out the way, and witness free, hopefully. He drove the industrial estate through its heart and out the other side to the last tendrils of roads, where the very remnants of business lay. He drove down a cul-de-sac, Marshal Road, an old tire place, defunct on the corner.

At the end of the road, Alex pulled the car through the gates of a ramshackle factory. The gates were open, as they had been when he'd scouted the place a few days ago, hung half off their hinges. The old chain link fence had holes in it. The building, he knew, was just as secure. After he'd parked up, Alex looked at Rush, still lost in his own little world of toy mittens. He was clearly *special*.

"Hey, Champ, how you doing?"

The boy looked up from his game and smiled in the mirror at Alex. "Where's Mummy?" he asked again.

Alex pointed at the building they were parked in front of. "She's in there. We're going to perform a trick for her. Won't that be fun?"

The boy frowned. "Like a magic trick?"

Alex nodded. "Yeah, Champ. Like a magic trick. You wait here, and I'll go get it ready, and then you can come in and we'll perform."

The boy made some cheering sound, before losing himself back into whatever game he was playing in his head. He didn't seem all that together for a six year old. Alex got out the car and went around to the boot, retrieving a holdall. He closed the boot and pressed the button on the fob to lock the door. While the kid wasn't smart enough to make a break for it—Alex doubted he was smart enough to open the door without a diagram—this wasn't a great area, and he would have hated for someone to grab the kid. *That would cause all sorts of fucking problems.*

He went into the building through the unlocked reception door and out the back to the factory floor. There, in the centre of the room was the trick. An old magician's box that would be used for fake-sawing his assistant in half to wow the audience. It was originally a simple device that relied on the assistant cocking their legs up under their chin and poking fake feet out the bottom. Alex dropped his bag next to it and pulled out a pair of black gloves, putting them on.

He took the handcuffs that he had brought with him from the bag and placed them on top of the magician's box, which itself sat on a table. There was nothing else in the room.

The table.

The box.

The handcuffs.

Alex checked the corners of the factory floor to make sure that there hadn't been any interlopers in the last few hours, particularly anyone that might still be there. Kids, most likely, meth heads. *Witnesses*.

Satisfied, he lay the holdall under the table and returned to the car.

He unlocked it and opened the door, sticking his head in the back to Rush. "Okay, Champ. Ready?" He didn't wait for the boy to stop playing, or even acknowledge him. Alex reached over and unhooked the kid's belt, and lifted him like a dead weight from the car. "Mummy's inside, waiting in the back for us to get ready."

The kid just squealed, "Mummy!"

Fucking hell.

Alex carried him into the building and through to the back, setting him down to walk on his own once they were on the factory floor. He took his hand and led him to the box. The boy looked at it with some sort of retarded wonder on his face. "What is it?" he asked.

"Magic box." Alex let go of his hand. "Magic box does magic things."

"Like what?"

"You'll see." Alex took the cuffs from the top of the box. "Like an escapist, yeah?" The boy giggled, understanding the next step in the magic trick and thrusting his hands out like he'd just been caught bang to rights on CSI. Maybe that was it? Maybe he'd been jammed in front of the TV for too long. Like, fourteen hours a day every day for the last six years? Alex slapped the cuffs on the kid. They weren't real hand cuffs. Firstly, Alex didn't want to waste the money on a real pair that he wasn't going to get back, and secondly, he expected the kid would be able to slip a pair of adult *proper* cuffs with his tiny, weird, child-sized wrists. Having met this particular kid, he'd given him too much credit. This kid probably couldn't get out of a chair without help. Either way, he'd picked up a pair of sex cuffs. Not proper BDSM things either. Pink fluffy shit that looked like they'd break if you twisted them hard enough.

And now the kid was wearing them, he was starting to look like a midget hooker, but it still wasn't helping him want to fuck him.

Alex smiled, and stopped himself from laughing. The kid probably wouldn't get the joke. He bent down and lifted the kid into the box. It was like putting a squirming cat in a coffin. Putting the kid's hands above his head, he locked the cuffs into place on the top of the box and closed the lid of it, over the kid.

Rush screamed, having been plunged into darkness.

Alex opened the flap revealing the kids face. "Is

Mummy watching now?" he asked.

"Sure." Alex looked down on the poor kid. Perhaps this was for the best. The kid was a simpleton, plain as day. He crouched down to access the bag under the table and as he did the kid started giggling. *Jesus Christ.* He opened the holdall and pulled out a multi-purpose saw. One he'd picked up in a hardware store in a small village about a hundred miles south of here. Unbranded. Untraceable. He stood.

The kid was staring at him. "Mummy?" he called, waiting with a look of expectation for the response.

"Wait there." Alex sighed and closed the lid. He flexed the saw like a wobble board in the hands of some legendary pervert that he couldn't remember the name of. *Wob-wob.* He grinned. "And now comes the screaming." He could hear the kid breathing irregularly in the box anyway, and probably about to start bawling again because he didn't like the dark. *Well, get ready for this.* Alex slid the teeth of the blade into the slit in the box in the centre. It was part-perforated to allow for the magician's easy sawing action, and so when Alex drew back the brand new sawblade, it slipped through to the kid's skin like butter. He held it there, feeling the weight of the blade on the boy. The boy, who hadn't noticed the impending pain.

With it supported by the slit in the box, Alex pushed the saw hard forwards, jaggedly cutting into the child. It slipped through his clothes, probably ripping them, rather than cutting them, and then bit at his skin, tearing into his flesh. Well, that was what Alex was imagining was happening—not that he could see.

Then the kid started howling. It was an interesting sound, something like an ambulance raping a pig violently and without lube. Then came the scream of *Muuuuuuum*.

Blood started to pool with vigour on the table below the box.

Alex took in a deep breath and pulled the saw back, feeling the blade swoop into the boys guts and pushed, digging it deeper. The little cunt stopped making all noise pretty quickly. *Good.* Alex left the saw hanging out of the side of the box, and breathed in once. The stink of iron and stomach acids was in the air. He breathed out and opened the flap to check Rush was dead. He was staring lifelessly outwards, with a few flecks of blood on his face as they had splashed up, inside the box. Alex closed it again. He pulled the two halves of the box apart, like the magicians would, but rather than spin them around with his assistant waving gleefully at an audience, the kid's insides slooped out of the two halves of his body onto the table beneath.

Alex looked at each half in turn. He really should fuck part of it at least, and this was more appealing than when the kid was alive. He ran his finger in a circular motion around a hole in the bits of Rush that were still inside the top half of his body like he was making a crystal glass sing. Or it was a hookers arse. He gently inserted his finger to gauge depth and lubrication. It was still warm, whatever it was. Maybe an intestine. He glanced to the bottom half of the body. The same opening was there too.

Neither were getting him hard.

It was very unprofessional to leave a job incomplete.

He stepped back from the table, wiping his finger on the kid's ragged clothes and scraped his feet on the hard concrete to make sure he didn't have any kid innards on him. "Aw, fuck." He looked under the table at the holdall that was sitting in Rush-goo. He was going to keep that. He'd picked it up from a motorway service station—charging Jones as an expense—but he'd quite liked it. It was rather natty. Well, bollocks. It was staying now. He wasn't about to risk physical evidence because of a bag.

Maybe he could pick up another one on the way back home.

He pulled out his burner phone and speed dialled Rush's father—the only number in the phones memory. "It's done," he said when Jason Jones answered. "Never mind where. It's best you don't know. I've rigged it up to look like a Gacy copycat. Except I sawed him in half. Shit. Sorry, I didn't mean to tell you that. Forget I said anything. But I didn't fuck him." Alex fell silent listening to Jason. "No … Gacy used to. Part magic trick, part sex show, but I didn't fancy doing the kid, though. Little retard probably wouldn't have noticed anyway—" Jones's voice got louder. "It's all part of the copycat thing … but I did fuck your wife." Then there was shouting. "What? She was the one who was fucking around town and got herself impregnated. I thought you'd be happy?"

He clearly wasn't.

"Well," Alex interrupted, "what are you going to do about it? Leave a bad Yelp review? I have records of you hiring me to murder your bastard son. I threw in the bitch as a freebie." Jones started crying. "It's all right," Alex said, soothingly. "I killed her too, so there's nothing tying it to you." The crying got louder. It was lucky that he'd already been paid, because this wasn't going in the right direct, and Alex's business wasn't one that tended to go to small claims court. "Anyway," he continued as Jones cried. "Gotta go. Please do give me a shout if there's anything else I can do." He doubted there would be.

All said and done, Alex rarely had repeat business due to the nature of it, but it didn't hurt to let people know he was available. It's not like he had business cards.

Maybe he should have business cards?

CHAPTER 3

Alex left the estate and hit the motorway going south. He'd lose the burner in the services at the bottom of the M1. Then there would be nothing tying him to the killings, except Jones himself, and he'd be a fool to let on. He'd spend nearly as much time in the big house as Alex would. A few times, when the job looked to be going pear shaped at the end of it—usually because the client was having cold feet—he'd thought about disposing of the last of the evidence, but if it got out that he was taking out the client, it'd be bad for business.

It'd all began when Alex had opened *Coles Investigations*. It was a simple set up. He'd rented an office just off the High Street in Ashbury—one of the cathedral and University cities in Kent, slapped a sign on the window and waited for the jobs. It was going to be like in the movies. He was going to have dames in the office, slathering all over him because they thought their husbands were fucking their secretaries and Alex was going to tail them and snap them in the act, like some shitty porno photographer, except with more hiding, and more sexual perks from overly thankful wives and girlfriends.

Except, not so much.

He barely managed to scrape the rent together, even living in the office. He started to stink a little too, what with there being no shower there. Once, he'd tried to use the showers at the Uni swimming pool, but he'd gotten his times all fucked up and ended up naked in front of a teenage swim team. He could have lied and said there was a happy ending, but alas, not. But that was a different story.

Anyway, just as being on the brink of bankruptcy was about to close the door for the last time, Alex was sitting in his office, with his thumb up his arse—metaphorically—, when a relatively well to do looking guy comes in. He was probably in his forties. Pot belly. He was wearing a suit that to a trained eye betrayed the air of money he was giving out. It was more Sainsbury's chic, than Saville Row. The guy introduced himself as Roger Smith, but pronounces it Sm-high-th. Twat. He said that he thought his wife was cheating on him, and that he wanted some evidence.

Alex jumped at finally having a proper job.

Smith handed over all the details and gave Alex a week to come up trumps with the evidence. So Alex jumped straight on the case without a second thought. He took his private investigator camera (in hindsight, he should have just used the camera on his phone and spent the money on food), and staked out the Smith's house. All he had to work on was the photo Smith had left with him and a name. *Sharon*. Now, in the photo, Sharon looked a little younger than Smith, and even Alex had to admit that this dude was punching well above his weight. Their house was on the outskirts of the city and Alex took up residence in the car opposite.

His wealth of detective experience was coming

from re-runs of Magnum P.I. and old movies. A little Murder She Wrote.

The first look he got at Sharon told him an abundance of information. For a start this chick was way younger than Smith. A good ten years. She was also hot. Not super-model shit-hot, but hot like most men leaving puberty up to the age of death would bang her without thought. So Alex tailed her. Barely three days in, and Sharon was disappearing into a hotel in the city centre, with obvious connotations. She was banging someone in there.

Only thing was, Alex couldn't get a looksy inside a decent and reputable joint like that. So he goes back to Smith and reported: Sharon is banging men in the hotel in the centre.

Smith was doubtful.

So he asked Alex if there is any way he can get evidence of her banging some other bloke, maybe he could get her in a compromising position himself? Now this intrigued Alex, but he felt that it was a little unethical. Against some code of conduct that he had yet to learn, being a shit detective and all. So Smith all but threw more money at him. His work to date had rolled Smith three hundred quid—which had Alex creaming in his pants, what with being able to pay the rent and all—but then Smith intimates that Alex should screw his wife ... for another thousand. And take photos, if possible.

This was all starting to sound like Alex was being invited to an over paid porn shoot, and he was most certainly okay that.

Alex followed Sharon for a few more days,

discretely working out her routine. She seemed to be a lady of leisure, going to bars and such at lunchtime and meeting with *the girls*. Sometimes Alex witnessed acts of flirtation. Nothing major. Then she would go to the hotel in the centre and spend the afternoon.

On the fourth day, Alex bought a new suit from Matalan—thirty quid including the tie—and wore it while tailing her, following her into the hotel. She went in, and straight to the bar, where they seemed to know her, and she drank a cocktail.

Alex went to the bar and ordered a whiskey and dry. He had no idea what it was, but he'd seen his dad order it once, and it sounded classy. Tasted like shit, though. So he sipped his weirdly ginger flavoured whiskey and watched Sharon. She seemed to be taking her time, and certainly not actively seeking some sort of coupling. However, soon enough a guy came in. He went over to the bar and sat with her. They chatted briefly, she finished her drink and then she and this dude left.

Alex watched them go to the elevator in the lobby and in.

What the fuck?

With no explanation for the event other than he was living there—who the fuck lives in a hotel in the middle of a city?—or that she was the local bike and everyone knows *she who will fuck anybody from the bar*, Alex is a little stumped. He went over to the bar and slipped up onto the stool that she'd just left from. It was pleasantly warm. He beckoned over the barman. "I don't suppose you know where I might find some company for the night, do you?" he asked as slyly as he could. He realised that slyly came off as sleazy, but potato, potato, right?

The barman gave an involuntary little look to the lobby, before he said, "If Sir is looking for some action, Sir is out of luck for today." Then he winked at him.

Alex was taken aback that he was working as a detective in a sleazy shithole city without realising it. Smith's wife was hooking. In the best hotel in the city. Fuck.

Well, at least it made the next part of Smith's demands a little easier.

But his expenses were going to go up, that was for sure.

CHAPTER 4

Alex sat in the bar, on a stool, near where Sharon had sat the day previous. He'd already paid for a room for the night. There went three hundred of the thousand that Smith had given him upfront. He hoped he still had enough.

Giving the barman a nod in some stupid and somewhat childish attempt of saying, *why yes, I am looking for a prostitute*, he ordered a lemonade. No sense in impairing his performance, he assessed.

Then, as time went on—not even by that much— he scolded himself for not getting a whiskey. Why he was worried about his performance when he was about to screw a whore, he didn't know. Perhaps it was a professional concern. He wanted to look good in the photos, obviously. He was getting screwed up over nothing. Maybe he should order a proper drink.

No time for that.

Sharon walked in from the lobby, and headed over to a seat a few stools down from his. She was wearing a business suit that day. It gave her an air of one of those eighties movie dames, the ones that the rugged cop was going to fall for. A bit of rough, that sort of thing. She slipped onto the stool and the barman went straight to her, whispering something to her. She stood and came along the bar to Alex.

Christ. The barman was pretty much her pimp.

He wondered if he was getting a cut.

"Hi," she said, oozing onto the stool next to Alex.

"Why, hello," he replied. He came straight off as a fucking doofus.

"I believe you are looking for company?"

At least she was professional. "I am." Alex smiled at her.

"Two hundred for the hour, three thousand for the night."

Alex swallowed. *Seems reasonable*, he thought. "An hour?" He seemed unsure. "Maybe two?"

"Sounds good," she said. "What room are we in?"

Alex fumbled in his pocket for the key. He'd forgotten what room they'd given him. "Er, um." Fumble, fumble.

"There's no need to be nervous." She rested her hand on his hip.

Alex could feel himself getting hard. Shit. This was no time for his purity to get in the way. Sure, he'd *had* sex before. Just not a lot of it. *Not a lot.* Nowhere near enough. "Ah, here it is," he said, pulling the key from his pocket. "Two-eleven." She smiled and stood, taking his hand like they were a couple. They walked slowly, in silence, to the lift and she pressed the button, waiting. Alex was hyper-aware that all the staff in the hotel—the reception guy, the bell boy, that woman over near the door in a suit—they must all know he was about to hooker-up. *Damn.* He didn't want them to think that it was the only way he could get any tail.

Granted, in this current dry-spell—the last

eighteen months at least—it was, but that wasn't the point.

Then they were in the lift. More silence. He wasn't sure if he should speak. Should he make small talk? He looked her up and down as she waited for them to go up the two floors. She was slim. Ample breasts, but not huge. Blond hair in a pony-tail. *Ding*. The doors to the lift opened and she stepped out, leading him straight around to the left. She knew the place like the back of her hand. It was like she worked there.

Well, technically she did.

Alex raised a smile, but kept himself under control.

Within seconds they were in the room. It wasn't bad. Not much more than a Travel Lodge, bed, bathroom, desk, open fronted wardrobe. Mirror. Kettle.

Sharon cleared her throat.

Ah, yes. Alex realised he'd spent too much time admiring the room, and not the prostitute. "What would you like first?" she asked.

Having never been with a working girl before—that was it, *Working Girl*. She reminded him of Melanie Griffith—Alex wasn't sure of the protocol. Did she leave when he'd finished? Wham, bam, thank you, man? If that was the case, why was she asking what he wanted *first*? Did he get to finish as many times—oh, she was taking off his trousers. Alex guessed she gotten fed up waiting. He was thinking about this way too much.

His cock was hard before she'd gotten anywhere near it, and she had it in her mouth before Alex had even considered what he wanted *first*. This seemed good though.

Oh shit. He came. *Fuck*.

Sharon swallowed the lot without blinking before teasing the end of his cock with her tongue. She slid her mouth away from him. "Well," she said, sliding her arse back on the bed. "Wow."

Alex shuffled, embarrassed as he started to go flaccid. *Well, how am I getting photos now?*

Sharon looked at her watch. "We still have plenty of time," she said. "Let's see if we can't get you hard again."

Alex decided at that moment that prostitution should be legalised.

Sharon slipped from the bed like she was greased. "Take your clothes off and lay on the bed." She slipped silently into the bathroom and pushed the door to, but not closed. Alex could hear water running. He kicked his shoes off, flabbergasted that he'd finished up before he'd taken *those* off. Then his trousers, pants. He unbuttoned his shirt, fumbling, and managed to get on the bed without having a cardiac arrest. His heart was hammering.

He noticed his cock was hard again. Awesome job. Why was he congratulating himself? Who cared?

Sharon came out of the bathroom. She was wearing nothing but a pair of lace knickers. She admired his cock and ran her fingers over it. Before he knew it, she was on top of him, her knickers in his face, and she was playing with her tits. "You like this?" she was saying. She was grinning wildly. Either she was enjoying it, or she was a practiced actor. Alex pushed the memory of her being paid to do this to the back of his mind, and pretended she was enjoying it too. He wanted to reply, but couldn't find the words.

Photos. The thought kept nagging at the back of his mind. That, and *Oh God, I'm so hard I'm going to burst.*

Again.

Alex licked at her knickers, he really didn't know what else to do.

"Oh," she said. "You want that?" She got off him and stood next to the bed, sliding her knickers down and off. Alex slipped from the bed to allow her on, and she lay down, legs spread wide. Alex then buried his face in her snatch. It was well groomed and smelt nice. Which was something he concentrated on as he ate her out.

Next she got on her hands and knees and Alex was ploughing her from behind. She kept having loud, rolling orgasms—at least she *sounded* like she did. He hadn't realised he was that good in the sack.

As he was about to cum for the second time he pulled out, aware that he wasn't wearing a rubber. "Fuck," he muttered.

"What?" She wailed, moaning and groaning like he was Fabio or some shit. He was beginning to think she was putting it on.

"No johnny," he said.

"I don't care," she said. "Fuck me. Cum in me."

Urg. Alex suddenly remembered what the guy from yesterday looked like. He'd probably cum in her, maybe more than once. And she was there the day before that. And the day before *that*.

"Fuck me now," she demanded.

Suddenly, looking at the back of her head, all Alex saw was a cum-dumpster. Uh-oh. Flaccidity was returning. "I want to take your picture," he blurted. "As a memory."

Sharon rolled onto her back. "Another hundred," she said.

The illusion of him being a sexual god, and his masterful dick-work railing this gorgeous hunk of flesh to blood boiling orgasm time and again came crashing down. *Whore*. "No problem," he said.

"How do you want me?" She slid up the bed leaning her head against the headboard, and stuck two fingers up her twat.

Alex turned back to his suit, rumpled on the floor and pulled his detective camera from the inside pocket. He faced, her, slightly taken aback by her willingness to immediately be photographed and snapped her a couple of times, ensuring he got her face clearly in both. He thanked her, and then knew he had to take one for the team if he didn't want to raise suspicion.

CHAPTER 5

"As you can see …" Alex laid the photos across the desk. "… it's clearly her." He looked up at Roger, who was holding his face, staring through his fingers at the photos of Sharon, fingers up twat, in a hotel room.

"Did you fuck her?" he muttered.

"I don't think we need to discuss my methods." Alex smiled warmly at him, the memory of cumming over his wife's tits the previous afternoon still warming his cockles.

"I want you to kill her," he said, coldly.

"And a-what now?" Alex raised his eyebrows. "I don't think I heard you correctly."

"Kill her," he said. "Kill the fucking cunt."

"I think you should probably leave—"

"Here." Smith pushed his faux leather briefcase onto the edge of Alex's desk and popped it open. He pulled cash from inside and threw a wrapped pile of notes onto the photos. "Ten thousand."

Alex rubbed his chin. Part of him was nagging his conscience to throw the guy out of the office. This was disgusting. A total misappropriation of his skills, and totally unethical. The larger part of him was saying, *Mmmm. Ten thousand pounds. No more rent problems.* Alex reached forward and picked up the cash. "No backsies." Smith looked at him funny. "Sorry," he mumbled. "Well, I suppose, as you *are* a trusted client."

"But you listen," he said. "I want you to cut her up. Make it look like some dirty fucking client's gone psycho on her."

Alex thought about what Sharon had said yesterday, and said, "Another five thousand."

———

It had been surprisingly easy to get Sharon to leave the hotel. He'd met her that afternoon in the bar, and spun her a line about wanting to see her again but having to change where they could meet. She had agreed to see him in a couple of days at his new place. For the night this time. His work in the city had changed, he told her, and he was staying for a little longer, so he was renting a shabby maisonette on the outskirts of the city.

The actuality of it was that he had broken into the place, and was going to borrow it for the act. Simple.

Two days later, at seven in the evening, Sharon arrived and Alex let her in. He'd purchased a Chinese takeout and scooped it into bowls to increase the illusion of his potential infatuation. *Made* her a nice meal. They ate it quickly.

Honestly, it was pretty shit, but she seemed impressed that he had tried. *At least that was the impression she gave.* Then he led her through to the bedroom.

He'd done some research online and had gotten all the information he needed.

Sharon perched on the edge of the bed. "We've got all night," she said. "Why don't we spend a few minutes in here and then watch a film?" Alex was distracted, but he decided to let her suck his cock. And she *seemed* to enjoy doing it. He'd had enough of her shit now and wanted it done with. She wiped her lips with the back of her hand leaving a gross trail of lipstick behind on her cheek, before excusing herself to the bathroom, while Alex got the TV ready.

He went to the kitchen and start popping some popcorn in the microwave—one of those shitty three for a pound bags that did the job, but impressed no one—and took the cleaver from the knife block.

He'd driven out of the city and picked everything up that he'd needed earlier that day. The expenses were climbing, but he still had all of the ten thousand from Smith in his desk at the office. He made a mental note that he was going to need to get a safe if this sort of work continued. He slid the cleaver under the cushion on the sofa and flicked the TV onto a movie channel. Fucking *Die Hard* was just starting. Awesome.

Sharon came back and sat next to him. He put his arm up and around her shoulders like he was into her, and they might make out like they were at the movies. He was just biding his time. "Isn't there anything else on?" she asked.

Anything else? Alex thought about grabbing the cleaver and finishing it there and then. Die Hard? Anything else? Fucking hell. "Like?" he asked.

"Something more sexy," she said, taking the remote and flicking through the channels.

There's nothing sexier than John-Fucking-McClane dropping fools out of windows, bitch.

She rose through the Freeview channels like a pro, until she got to the adult channels in the high numbers. Luckily, whoever actually owned this pad was schmoe enough to be paying for fucking porn channels, as they weren't encrypted. What a loser. The Internet's free, right?

Two girls were banging on the screen, yelping and squealing like fucking anime characters.

"You like that?" Sharon asked, slipping her hand into Alex's trousers. With her jiggling him about and the lesbian's sixty-nining on the TV, he was getting a little up. Then Sharon pulled his cock out and leaned down onto it, taking it into her mouth again.

A very small part of Alex wanted to off her in the morning, rather than now. This could be an interesting night, however, he really needed to get it done, and get out, before anything went wrong.

He kept his hand rested on the back of her head as she bobbed up and down, while he fished for the cleaver under the cushion. He needed her to be off him, before he struck, though. The last thing he needed was to have her bite his dick off when he cleaved her in twain. Then she pulled up and off, before he had it out. The cleaver, not his cock.

"Tie me up and fuck my arse," she said, grinning wildly at him.

Alex nodded, silently, as the two of them returned to the bedroom. While Sharon stripped naked, surprisingly quickly—maybe she was actually getting into this?—Alex fished around in the wardrobes looking for something to restrain her with.

She lay face down on the bed and Alex used two of the schmoes ties to restrain her to the bedpost. She had her arse sticking up in the air. Alex quickly weighed some of the pro's and con's. He'd never done anal. That was a pro. He was about to hack her up, though. Probably a con.

He decided against it.

Alex hurried to the living room and retrieved the cleaver.

"What's the hold up?" she asked. For a prostitute, she seemed awfully impatient. Alex looked from the cleaver to her and back again. He should have just hacked the cleaver down into her and got the job over with, but he wasn't quite ready yet. Stage fright, perhaps. Thinking quickly he sucked his index finger and then jammed it into her arsehole. She squealed and laughed and he withdrew it, hoping that would sate this awful wench of a woman for a few moments.

This was all getting out of hand.

He felt the weight of the cleaver in his hand, his attention drawn to Sharon moaning in some weird ecstasy even though he was nowhere near her. Perhaps it was for the best, because at that second Alex lost his temper and straddled across her arse. She made a cooing sound and he raised the cleaver up, above his head. He'd seen films. This shouldn't be hard.

She was still making gooey noises like he was fucking Valentino or something. He tilted his head to the side. *No wonder she was so popular.*

Alex dropped the cleaver down like the executioner slinging the axe, except Alex slammed the blade into the bad of Sharon's head, splitting it in two. The weight of the blade, the strength of his thrust—he'd never know which—caused the cleaver to slide straight through Sharon and into the mattress below. He even let out a surprised little *eep*.

CHAPTER 6

With her head split in two, Alex lifted the cleaver back up and looked at it like it held magic powers. Fucking Excalibur. Or He-Man's sword, whatever that was called. He looked down at Sharon, fragments of bone and goo slipping and sliding across what was left of her brain.

Her body twitched.

Alex jumped, the memory of Romero's zombies rising to the forefront of his mind, before he scrambled to the side of the bed. He let out a laugh, uncontrollably. *Zombies*. His heart was beating hard, and he could feel the adrenaline rushing through him. What now? He shook his head, trying to get himself straight.

Smith had already paid him, but he should collect some sort of evidence. He tossed the cleaver on the bed and went through to the hallway, doing his trousers back up as he went. Damn it. He looked at the floor. He was bare foot. There must be physical evidence fucking everywhere. Still, no time for that.

He got his detective camera out of his rucksack by the front door and went back to the bedroom. He snapped a photo of Sharon where she was laying, then looked at the picture. The head area was a bit blurred, or maybe that was her brains spewed out over the sheets? Surely if Smith asked, he'd know that this was her, just from the back of her body? He must know what his wife looked like?

Hold on. In a couple of days the police would find her and contact Smith. Then he'd know.

Still.

He should get a better photo. Alex put the camera on the bed next to the cleaver and untied Sharon. He pulled her across the bed and then rolled her over onto her back. Her head flopped open. There was brain everywhere. "Fuck it." Alex could feel the vomit roiling about in his stomach. The fucking shit Chinese was coming back with a vengeance. He swallowed it down. *Physical evidence*, he thought, over and over.

Alex pushed the two halves of Sharon's head back together and tried to balance them so that he could get the camera, but they kept wanting to flop open. He lost his temper, and stormed back into the living room, pacing back and forth. "Stupid fucking cunt ... glad she's dead." He stopped, and looked around the room. His eyes fell on the schmoe's desk. Opening the drawers he found a roll of sellotape.

Fucking hallelujah.

He went back into the bedroom and spun the tape around and around the top of Sharon's head until the two halves stayed in place. She was still lop-sided, but she was definitely recognisable. He took the photo.

Standing there in the bedroom, he found himself admiring the ludicrousy of the situation. She was taped up, like some macabre mummy figure and naked. This was how the police would find her.

Or more likely, the schmoe. Who would need counselling, *possibly for years*.

Alex started to laugh. He roared with laughter until tears streamed from his face and he was bent over in two and slapping his thighs. "Fucking hell," he whimpered through the tears.

Then the vomit came. Right there on the rug in the bedroom. Partially digested chop suey spewed onto the shag, along with mushrooms and bits of chicken. There was sweetcorn too, which was weird because he hadn't had any sweetcorn for days.

Well, he thought, *there's always sweetcorn, isn't there? So much for physical evidence.* He tutted. Never mind.

Alex collected up his detective camera and the cleaver, and put them away in the backpack. He thought about cleaning up the sick, then decided, being as his cum was in her, he had pissed earlier, and touched just about everything, there seemed little to no point.

He was probably going to jail for this.

And Hell. He was definitely going to Hell.

Hell would probably come up later, but the police did such a shit job when the body was found three weeks later, that his DNA being absolutely everywhere was missed completely.

And that was how it all began.

CHAPTER 7

Alex opened the door in the corridor that led to his offices and scooped up the post from behind it. He'd been up north on the Jones case for a week or more. He closed and locked it behind him. He was tired and wasn't planning on seeing anyone else today. He went through into his office, and pushed the door to.

He punched the number into the safe that sat on the floor behind the door and opened it, dropping in the thirty thousand that Jones had paid him for the kid. He charged a lot for kids. Most people wouldn't touch them. But Alex would.

He slammed the safe closed and went to the desk dropping the post down and sitting. He got the half empty bottle of whiskey from the bottom desk drawer, and the single glass that sat in there, and poured himself a healthy shot of the brown liquor. He pressed the button on the old fashioned answer phone and let the messages play through. Most of them were from Jax Sheldon. She was his pimp—for lack of a better term.

Most of Alex's work came from strange sources. The dark web? Yeah, sure, why not? A4 hand written posters in phone boxes? Not so much anymore, but again, yeah. Twitter? That too. But he couldn't keep up with it, so he hired Jax. She was his secretary, probably. He paid her well, and she kept the looney's from him. He picked up a pen and pulled his notepad over to him. Jax would call and leave him the job, the pay, and the serial number she had assigned it.

Apparently he needed to be this organised. Then he could call her back with the codes and she could give him the full details of the job.

She had several jobs left over several messages. Someone wanted their wife killed. Someone else wanted their neighbour broken into. Some chick wanted to fuck a dangerous man—he wrote that code down. The last message from Jax was about a guy who wanted help with something called *Kuman Thong*. Sounded weird. Alex was about to delete the message when Jax said that he should Google it, and that the guy was willing to pay *very well*.

Alex wrote down the code and then deleted the message.

———

"Gross." Alex finished flicking down the Wikipedia page. Then he pressed the print button, and the laser printer sparked to life, spewing pages out to the desk. He picked his phone up and dialled Jax.

"Morning." She sounded chipper as usual. "Whatcha decided on?"

"Good morning. I had a lovely week up the road, thank you. Code F56, and Code O34."

"No surprise there." Jax jotted down the code for the woman who wanted to have sex with a dangerous man. "Did you look up the uh … what was it … Kuman Thong?"

"Yeah. What's the pay?"

"He wants three, and …" There was a flicking of

papers. "… he's willing to drop seven thousand on each one."

"Doesn't seem like much. Look, I couldn't get much information from the Internet. How old do they need to be?"

"From what I could gather from the client, between four and five months."

Alex nodded, scribbling it down. "And the gold coating? Is that an expense?"

"Sure to be. Do you want his number?"

"Yeah, okay. And the other one."

Jax gave him the two names and the two numbers. Alex wrote them down and politely got rid of Jax. She was good at her job and thoroughly professional, and sometimes Alex didn't want that. Sometimes he wanted a chat. He knocked back the rest of the glass of whiskey and then topped it up. It was only nine in the morning, but who gave a fuck? When you were dealing with people like this, being half cut first thing in the morning wasn't such a bad thing. He looked at the two numbers. He wanted to call the woman first and find out how she wanted this *dangerous man thing* played out, but he knew that if he went down that rabbit hole first he was unlikely to emerge for a week, and the other job was going to pay more. Especially after he'd negotiated a new price.

He took a deep breath and dialled the man's number.

"Hello?" The man sounded Asian, which wasn't really a surprise, given the name Jax had him write down.

"Mr Chaisai?"

"It's just Chaisai. I take it this is Alex Cole. You have my request."

"I do. Look, I'll be honest. This is all a little weird. You're going to have to run me through some of the finer points."

"I didn't think it was that complicated, Mr Cole. I want three four month old human foetuses emblazoned in gold."

"Yeah. You see, that's the thing. According to my research they need to be cooked, right?"

"Yes."

"Okay. And fresh?"

"Yes."

"And covered in gold."

"Yes."

"For twenty one thousand."

"Yes."

Alex looked at the woman's number and wished he'd called that one instead. "Human," he muttered to himself. "I need eleven thousand for each kid. You know, if you want me cutting these things outta people, that's going to cost." The line went quiet. He had Chaisai on the ropes. "And then there's the cost of the gold …" he let the words hang in the air.

"Eleven. No expenses."

Alex tapped his pen on the desk. "Okay. I'm in. But I gotta ask, what the fuck do you want them for?"

"The ritual using the golden sacrifice is ancient and legendary. It is for the black arts, Mr Cole. That is all you need to know."

"Okay, fine. I'll get on it. I take it that I can refrigerate them once they are ... prepared? And you'll want all three together?"

"Yes, Mr Cole."

"Okay. I'll take this one as cash on delivery, given that I want to keep as much distance between me and you as is humanly possible right now. Please be aware though, that in this business my word is my contract, and should you break contract from this conversation onwards, there will be fatal ramifications."

"I understand, Mr Cole. I look forward to your call once you have the merchandise." Chaisai ended the call.

Merch. Wow. Even Alex was surprised at the coldness. Still, he'd been asked to do worse. But not much. This was new, at least. *Cuttin' babies outta mothers*. He picked up the phone and dialled the woman's number. Take his mind off this job for a few minutes.

"Yes?" She sounded horny already and Alex hadn't spoken yet.

"Miss Donna Philips?"

"Missus. Yes, that's me." She huffed the words out like a phone sex operator.

"My name is Cole. I believe you spoke with my colleague, Jax? You were looking for a service."

"Well, I've never heard it called that before." She giggled. This was going to be easy money. "I want a real man, for a change, and you seemed to be right up my alley, so to speak."

Alex nodded. "Indeed. I've got to clear up a couple of the details though. I assume that you're going to need me to produce some evidence that I am a *dangerous man*, as you put it?"

"I'll leave that up to you. The more dangerous you are, the better time you'll have."

Alex wrote *take a foetus* next to her name and underlined it. "And you didn't discuss payment terms with my colleague."

"What are you worth, Mr Cole?"

"Every penny." He smiled to himself. "But you're married right? Look I'm not going to charge extra for the evidence that you're asking for, but if there is a likelihood that I'm going to get entangled with a pissed off husband, I'm going to need insurance."

"I'm a widow, Mr Cole. You have nothing to worry about, except bringing your a-game."

"Huh." Cole scribbled down some numbers. "Where about are you?"

"London. I'd like you at my place, so that I can feel safe."

"Seems reasonable." He sketched down travel, time, effort. Then he ran a line through effort. He probably shouldn't charge for that. "How does a thousand sound? Let's call it a new customer deal."

The woman thought for a second and then agreed. "Not a problem, Mr Cole. I'm eager to move forward. When are you available?"

Alex looked at the map of the country pinned to the corkboard on the wall. He just needed to get the evidence first. If he got the first foetus from London, clean it up, maybe cook it? Then … "How about I give you a call in a couple of days? Do you need notice?"

"Oh no, Mr Cole."

"Call me Alex. I'll speak to you soon."

CHAPTER 8

Alex sat in the flat he'd rented under the name *Ronnie Driscol*. It was a name he'd used before, he already had the IDs and everything, so it was an easy base to make in London for a week. He was watching the TV. Smith had reported his son missing and his wife had been found dead. Everything seemed to be going to plan. He left the flat at about nine in the morning, wanting to miss the heavy traffic, and driving to the nearest hospital—one with a maternity wing.

He sat in the car park—rental car, obviously—and watched the mothers come and go. He was trying to work out how he could tell the age of the babies by sight. He needed a label. Or a baseline. Something. Some of the bumps were huge—probably babies ready to drop—some barely showed—too young—or was it that some babies were fat? Alex shook his head and got out of the car. He wandered around the car park for some time wishing he had never given up smoking.

He supposed he should approach one of the women and strike up a conversation. He could do that. He watched a woman waddle from her car towards the building. The only thing was, that he was used to chatting with women with an undertone of sexuality in the conversation. Surely these women wouldn't want that? *Oh my God*, he thought. He'd forgotten how to speak to women without flirting with them.

A woman with a mid-sized bulge came out of the

front door and staggered over to a covered waiting area. Probably the old smoking shack, before they'd made it illegal to smoke on hospital premises. She looked exhausted. Alex walked over to her and sat next to her. "You okay?" he asked. He stared straight ahead, the likelihood of him flirting was lower if he didn't look her in the eyes.

"Yeah," she said. She patted the side of her stomach. "This little fucker keeps giving me a kicking, is all." She laughed. "Excuse my French," she said.

Alex joined in with the laugh. "Don't worry about that. How old is the little fucker?"

"Five months," she said.

Fucking hell. A stroke of luck. And he now knew that babies were kicking at that age. Foetuses. Whatever. The more you know, right? The woman started to her feet. "Can I help?" he asked.

"You're okay. I'm just going to the bus stop." She held her weight on the seat.

Alex got up, and held her arm, taking her weight on that side of her body. "You can't get a bus in this state. Why don't you let me give you a lift?"

The woman looked at him. He could see part of her wanted to say yes, but the other part was sure he was a serial killer. "I've just dropped my sister off, and she won't be ready for hours," he lied. "I can give you a lift home—you'd be there in no time."

She smiled slightly.

"Come on, I don't bite," Alex said, standing. He introduced himself as Ronnie, and she responded. Her name was Ashley. Alex helped her over to the car and got her in. He chosen a mid-sized family car from the rental place. It seemed like a reasonable choice at the time, and now, as he fell further into his character, it seemed perfect. He tried not to get too handsy with her as he helped her in. This had to be her first kid, based on how little free movement she seemed to have, and how much she moaned and groaned about everything. Getting her in, he managed to get more of a handle on the sort of woman she was. She was young—twenty-five-ish—and more cute than pretty. She was wearing oversized clothes, and between that and the bump it was hard to tell what her natural physique was like. She started to struggle to put the belt around her as he closed the door.

Alex went around to the driver's side. He couldn't believe his luck this early into the game. He jumped in, and turned the engine on, pushing the *On* button on the GPS. "Where are we heading?" he asked. His excitement had him a little flustered.

"I thought I was the pregnant one," she said. She beamed at him, and Alex felt a small pang of attraction. It was true what they said—she *was* glowing.

"Heh." He did his best to get himself together. "Gotcha."

"Station Road," she said. "SE24."

Alex punched in the postcode and drove out of the hospital. The voice on the machine told him where to go, and just followed it, blindly. Ashley would let him know if he was going the wrong way. It was only a couple of miles away, anyway. *Great.* "So

…" Alex struggled to find a suitable question to ask. He should know this. Damn it. He hadn't done his homework properly. He could have kicked himself. He was *supposed* to have a pregnant sister. "…finding it hard around the home?" It was shit, but it was something.

"Yeah," she said. "I mean, my mum tries to help where she can, but she's not always there." She stared out the window. "I would be nice to have a hand every now and again."

"It must be difficult."

"I could have done with a husband."

Alex could hear the pout in her voice. "Sorry," he said. "I don't mean to pry."

"It's fine." She rubbed her belly. "One night stand, and he didn't want anything to do with the little fucker. I mean, what a prick."

Alex smiled to himself. "Nearly there," he said, watching the GPS. He pulled off the main road and into a one way street.

"Down here on the left," she said, like he was taxi driver.

Alex pulled into a narrow space. The houses were terraced. The road was narrow. He was going to have to be quiet. He wasn't expecting to get his first like this. It was like mana from Heaven. He popped off his seatbelt and got out the car, going around to her side and opening the door.

Like a real gent.

She struggled out and Alex tried his best to help

without being too grabby. He didn't want her to get any creep vibes from him. She smiled at him, as he took her hand, helping her across the curb. "I don't suppose you have time for a coffee?" she asked. "To say thank you."

Alex glanced at his watch and nodded. "It would be an honour."

CHAPTER 9

Alex sat at the dining table in the kitchen while Ashley made tea. Bags in cups, he noted. The table had one of those plastic table cloths on it—like you would have for a kids fucking party. It went with everything else he'd seen. She was broke. That was clear. The décor in the house was pretty worn, the carpet was damaged in a couple of places. It stank of being a rental. The landlord must be a right cunt too, treating a pregnant woman with this level of disrespect. Her furniture all looked second hand, and not second hand in the *I bought it from a reputable purveyor*, sort of way, and more *hand me downs from neighbours*, sort of way. The cups were chipped. She was talking away about nothing in particular, which was just as well, because Alex wasn't really listening. He was too busy *detectiving*.

She turned and put the tea down in front of him. It was milky. Weak as shit, and she'd already taken the bag out. What the fuck? Deep in Alex's stomach anger stirred. The cheek of inviting him in to give him piss-tea. "So you live alone?" he asked.

She nodded. "Yep." She sat down at the table opposite him. "Just me and LF. I've got the council paying the rent, and it's a two bed, so while it's just me and him, we've got plenty of space."

"Him?"

"Yeah. I wanted to know. I started to paint his bedroom blue, but I got bored and it's only half done."

Alex nodded. "Mind if I see it?" He glanced around pretending to be embarrassed. "I'm just looking for ideas. I've been trying with my …" He wasn't wearing a wedding ring. "… partner."

Ashley smiled. "Of course." She pointed at the ceiling. "You don't mind if I don't show you?" She rested her hands on her belly. "He's heavy."

Alex smiled and got up from the chair. "Not at all. Where am I going?"

"First door on the left."

Alex nodded, left the kitchen and went up the stairs. There were only two doors at the top. The bathroom must have been downstairs somewhere. He pushed the door on the right open and looked into Ashley's bedroom. Small. Double bed, unmade. Clothes all over the floor. Not only did she live alone, she didn't have a lot of company. Even better. There was less chance of someone coming around without warning. He pushed the door on the left open and stuck his face in. Yes. Blue. Half painted. He went back downstairs. Returning to the kitchen he noted that there was a door out the back of the kitchen which must be the bathroom, and he looked out the window into the back garden. It was a small space. Patch of grass, and a small shed. It was more of a yard.

Ashley was smiling at him.

Alex thought she might have just been glad of the company. He let his gaze drift around the kitchen, taking in his surroundings without looking like he was inspecting her stuff. There were one or two handy items. He eyed the cooker. It looked pretty clean, if not a bit shit. At least that was something.

"So are you happy?" Ashley suddenly asked.

Alex looked at her, surprised. He sat back down and picked up his tea. "Um … yeah?" He squinted at her. "Why do you ask?"

"It just that …" She picked up the spoon that was sitting next to her mug. "… well, it seems strange for a man to want to help me out of the goodness of his heart. I just thought that you might …" Her words drifted off. "… Silly, really." She looked down at herself, and patted the bulge again. She sniffed up some snot.

She was crying.

"What?" Alex was taken aback. "I-I didn't realise. I'm sorry."

"No," she said. "I know I'm fat and ugly now." She tossed the spoon on the table. "You probably want to go. I'm sorry. I'm so fucking stupid."

"Don't be silly." Alex stood up and went around the table to her. He crouched next to her and took her hand. "Believe me, you've still got it. You are one sexy lady, and you don't think otherwise, you hear me?"

She looked at him and started to lean in to kiss him. Alex responded. He pushed his lips against hers, raising his hand to her cheek and wiping away the tears. Staring into her eyes he pulled away. The spark was back. The one he'd seen in the car, but missed the meaning. He stood back up and went around behind her, massaging her shoulders. "It can't be easy," he said. "You must be lonely. Desperate, to want a wreck like me."

She tried to look around to his face. "Not at all. I … wanted you as soon as I saw you." She giggled coquettishly.

Alex kept one hand on her shoulder and reached over to the counter with the other, unseen by Ashley. He picked up the toaster. *Urg.* It was all greasy. Fuck. Who uses a greasy toaster? It's a fucking fire hazard. He raised it above his head and smacked it down as hard as he could on the top of Ashley's head. There was a thud and small spray of blood as her skull cracked under the force. He raised it back up for a second hit, letting go of her shoulder, but she flopped, forehead first onto the table. Alex pushed his fore and middle fingers into her neck and felt a pulse. She was still alive. Shit. He raised her head off the table, lifting it by her hair and took the cable of the toaster, wrapping it around her neck. She muttered and moaned a little, drifting between unconsciousness and awake as Alex pulled the cable taut and throttled the air from her. She didn't fight or scream. She just slumped, half-blacked out before he started, and gone in seconds.

Alex kept it pulled tight for a minute before releasing her and feeling for a pulse again. She was dead. Alex put the toaster back on the counter and wiped his greasy fingers down his coat. He pulled her chair away from the table and her corpse plunged to the floor. There was a hollow thud as her head hit the dirty tiles. Alex pulled the chair and table to the side of the room and pulled the window blinds down. There were no overlooking houses behind, but it would be just his luck for some nosey fucking neighbour to burst into the garden looking for a cup of sugar. He looked at the sugar bowl on the table. It had coffee grains—he hoped—mixed into the white stuff. *Good luck with that*, he thought. *Anyway*. He pulled her out flat on the floor by her feet. Alex stared at her belly.

He wondered how long the little fucker lived for after she was dead.

Alex worked his way around the drawers in the kitchen. He found a long bladed knife. That might do. He had tools in the car, but if he could avoid coming and going that would be safest. He just didn't want to be seen too many times. He took the blade, and got to his knees on the floor, spreading Ashley's legs and getting between them. He pulled her skirt tight and slid the blade through the fabric, slicing it open. It worked, but the blade was dull as fuck. He pushed her open skirt to the side, and slid the blade between her skin and her panties, pulled the blade towards himself and cut through the fabric. He pulled them from her body and sniffed at them, before tossing them to the corner. She smelled sweet. He wondered if that was her, or if it was because she expecting. He looked at her pussy. It looked like it was neatly shaved in the past, but it was growing back in. She probably couldn't reach it. He let himself look up her body. From this angle it was like he was worshipping her. Another time, another place, she would be tied to the bed, and he would be about to lick her to orgasm. He crawled up her a little to get a better angle, and he cut her oversized jumper from her. Then the t-shirt underneath—it was pulled tight across the bump. He pushed all her clothing from her and had access to the belly now.

Alex looked at her tits, hidden beneath a bra. It used to be white. It looked sort of clean, but had stains. He slid the knife under it and cut through the material. She was nude now, apart from the rags wrapped around her arms. Alex let his hand touch her breast. They were tight, bigger because of the pregnancy, perhaps. She had puffy nipples. He liked that. It would have been good for the kid.

Probably.

He pulled his attention back to her stomach. The plan was simple. Get the foetus out. He looked at the bulge, then the knife. He didn't want to puncture the baby and have to get a replacement. *Right. Think logically. Think like a handyman.* What was the easiest way in? Start with a hole? That was right. If she was a lump of wood, he'd drill a hole in her to get started.

Ah-ha.

Alex scooted down her body and lay almost flat between her legs, his face inches from her slit. He brought the knife up to her gash and slid it in, slowly. After he had the knife in a couple of inches, he pulled the knife upwards and started a sawing motion, trying to use the knife to open her up like a loaf of bread.

It seemed like a solid idea, but in practice, Alex was sawing against moist flesh and getting nowhere at all. All he seemed to have achieved was turning her cunt into chopped beef. "Fuck it," he shouted, yanking the blade out and chucking it across the kitchen against the front of the fridge. "Stupid poor bitch and your blunt fucking knife." He got up and slammed his hands down flat on the draining board, staring out the window.

"Ah," he blurted out, suddenly.

Alex unlocked the back door and stormed across the grass to the shed, swinging the door open. He looked around the sparse contents. "Of course," he said, standing on the shittest lawnmower he'd ever seen and reaching across. "Everyone's got some, and no one knows why." He pulled a rusted pair of hedge shears from a nail in the wall. He made the traditional dad manoeuvre and opened and closed them twice in quick succession, with them getting easier to close on the second time. They made the snip, *crack* sound to Alex's pleasure. "Great," he said, genuinely pleased with himself.

He returned to the house and closed the back door, getting back on the floor between her legs. He opened the shears and slid one blade up her fanny, and rested the other on her pubes. He wrangled it around a bit so that he didn't need to cut through the bone.

He was glad she was already dead, because she seemed nice, and he was making all sorts of mess in there, rearranging the furniture, as it were. He took a deep breath, before he ventured onto new ground. He didn't think this was going to happen this way, but what the hell? If it worked, he still needed another two. Practice makes perfect.

Breath held, he slammed the two handles back together.

The two blades slipped through the woman's skin with ease, and he did actually miss all the bone.

Blood squirted from her newly opened belly,

leaving Alex to wonder if the ball-shape of the belly was actually full of blood. It sprayed him across his shirt and face, making him look like he'd been bobbing for apples in a maths teachers ink pot. "Well," he said. Alex dropped the shears on the floor and grabbed each side of the belly, parting it like the red sea.

Inside was a formed human baby. It wasn't *finished*, as such. The head was a funny shape and it didn't have fully formed fingers, but it was close. *Cool*. The baby was contained within a sack or some shit, and there were cords and things that Alex vaguely remembered having to sit through in school. He got up and retrieved the knife.

When he got back on his knees he jabbed the end of it through the sack and a clear viscous liquid flowed out over everything, mixing with the blood and other, weird looking fluids that he'd discovered inside Ashley.

There, kneeling in a pool of bodily fluids, Alex reached down and retrieved the child from the sack, lifting it carefully, trying not to break it. Like it was a mint action figure.

Then the little fucker moved.

The sight of the baby voluntarily moving it's arm—more than likely it's death throe—made Alex drop it to the floor. It made a splooping sound because it was wet, bloody, slimy, and not particularly solid. "Jesus fucking Christ," he yelped, backing away. It didn't move again.

Alex nudged the little corpse with his shoe.

"Fuck."

He picked up the knife and managed—with some effort—to saw the umbilical cord away, and release little baby *LF* from his imprisonment.

Then he ran it under the tap washing the goo off. Bits of the inside of Ashley wetly plopped into the bottom of the sink. He lay the baby corpse on the draining board. Alex leaned down in front of the cooker. "Well," he muttered. "It would save time." He ran his finger along the knobs on the front and turned the oven onto fan. *Fan would work, right?* He looked at the child. Fuck.

Alex got his phone out and pulled up Google. He searched for *cooking time bone in shoulder of pork*. He couldn't actually search for what he was really looking for, now could he? The recipe he pulled up suggested some cooking times based on weight. He looked around the kitchen. Of course this poor arse drop-out didn't have any scales. He picked up the foetus and bobbed it up and down in his hand like he was Indiana fucking Jones. "Five hundred grams?" he muttered to himself. He was just guessing. He had no idea. He looked down the instructions.

An hour with guaranteed crackling. Fine.

His eyes drifted over to the salt and pepper pots on the table—the only herbs and spices this house had ever likely seen, then he shook his head. It's not like he was actually going to eat the thing, now was it? He rummaged around in the cupboards and found a shitty metal tray.

He oiled it, and popped the kid in the oven.

CHAPTER 10

Alex sat in Ashley's kitchen wearing nothing but his pants. He was fresh out the shower and watching the tumble dryer go around. The flavour of the foetus had filled the kitchen. It smelt a little like roasting, but bland. Unflavoured. But hey, he wasn't being paid to be a professional chef now, was he?

The dryer stopped and he pulled his shirt and trousers out, now free from Ashley goo. He slipped the warm clothing back on and looked at his watch. The baby roast should be finished soon. He dialled Donna Philips.

"Hello?" She sounded as sexy and sultry as she had on the phone the other day.

"Mrs Philips. Alex Cole. I was wondering if you'd be available?" Alex stood and pushed the phone under his chin, took a pair of oven gloves and took the tray with the baby on it from the oven. He hoped that Chaisai wanted it crispy. He assumed, being as he still had to *emblazon it with gold* that whatever it was for, it wasn't for eating. He probably should look that up tonight, when he'd finished for the day.

"I am," she replied. "Well, I can be. I'm in Knightsbridge, when would you like to come?"

Knightsbridge? Fancy. "I'm just the other side of the river, I can be there in say, an hour?"

"Fine." Donna gave him the address. "And don't forget your evidence," she said. He could hear the humour in her voice, but looked at the foetus. Ah well. What was the worst thing that could happen?

"I'll see you in an hour." Alex ended the call. He started going through the cupboard, hoping in vain to find a silver platter and cloche. Fat fucking chance. He ended up with a Tupperware box and lid that didn't match. He stuffed the bottom of it with kitchen towels and put the corpse on top, before covering it with more towels and then snapping the lid in place.

He left Ashley where she was on the floor of the kitchen, the pools of blood around her drying onto the tiles because of the heat in the kitchen. He left the cooker on low. The ambient heat in the room would distort the time of death. There was no way he was going to be able to hide the motive—he glanced at the lunch boxed baby—but he should get away with it.

Alex left, placing the Tupperware in the foot well of the passenger seat and pumping Philips' address into the GPS.

Fifteen minutes later he was on Lambeth Bridge, heading into the far more expensive side of the smoke. Across the bridge and into the nicer part of town, Alex parked up the side of the small park opposite the address he'd been given. He looked less likely to get a ticket there. Not that this was going to take that long.

Easy money.

He took the lunch box and strolled over to the houses. They were tall. Eleventh Century. Million pound flats and houses. Some of the most expensive properties in the world. And there he was. Shabby detective, shabbying down the road. Dead baby in a lunch box. How teenage him would laugh if he could see himself now.

Or not.

He climbed the steps to the front door. The address Philips had given him was a house. He rang the bell.

CHAPTER 11

When the woman answered the door, Alex doubted that she could be Philips. She was a widow, and this woman was barely a kid. Maybe it was her daughter? "I'm here to see Mrs Donna Philips," he said, looking past her into the house.

"Mr Cole," she said. He recognised her voice immediately.

Alex raised an eyebrow. "May I?" he gestured into the house. He wanted to get himself and the lunch box off the street. Especially in an area like this. Philips turned and walked away, down the hallway, leaving the door open for him. Alex watched her for a few seconds, his mind taken from getting off the street. She was wearing a pencil dress. Her hips wiggled like she was on the catwalk. Her hair was long. Black as the ace of spades. She had high cheek bones, and a perfect nose. Her legs were long, covered in some shear stockings. High heels. She was obviously somewhere in her early twenties, but she had an air about her of someone far more experienced. She exuded style and sophistication, money, and grace.

Something wasn't right, that was for sure. This chick could have anyone. *Anyone*. What the fuck would she be paying for a bum like Cole for? The detective in him told him to leave. He glanced down the street towards the park. He could be in the car and away in seconds. The dick part of him wanted to go in and see where it led.

He tried to justify it in his head. *Maybe she was just looking for a bit of rough?* Alex looked from the lunch box to the arse, slowly disappearing to the end of the hallway. He stepped in and closed the door behind him.

———

Philips stood at the end of the hallway and beckoned Alex forward, curling her forefinger over like she was scratching the chin of a cat. She didn't speak. Alex walked along the corridor admiring the cost of the place. The house alone was probably in excess of twenty-mil. There were oils on the walls, pictures of people that looked wealthy. Philips must have come from that side of the family, because the resemblance in the paints to her was strong. As he got closer, he said, "Alex, please. No need to be formal."

Philips smiled. "Donna," she said. "Please come in."

Alex handed her the lunch box. "Evidence, as requested. I'll need it back though."

Donna nodded, taking the box. Alex went over to the sofa and sat. He felt dirty in the room. He felt cheap. Everything in there, the bookcase, the wing-backed chairs, a glass topped coffee table with this month's Home and Country on it, was expensive. The room smelt like money. She slunk over to the chair opposite him and perched on the edge of it, keeping her knees together, proper lady-like. She popped the top of the lunch box off and placed the lid down on the arm of the chair. Moving the kitchen towel to one side she raised an eyebrow and smiled. She looked at him and cocked her head. "Takeaway," she said.

Alex was unsure if she knew what it was or not.

"I won't bother asking for the details of why, as I'm sure you are far too professional to divulge, but *why is there a dead baby in this lunch box*, does sound a little like an opening to a joke."

"No joke, I assure you." Alex smiled. "But as my client, can I just ask one question?"

"Shoot." She smiled. The word was unbefitting of her.

"Why? Why on earth do you want to bed me? I mean, I get that you didn't necessarily know what I looked like until only a moment ago, must you must have known you were running the risk of a schlub."

"You can see what I have, Alex. You can see that I want for nothing. Is there anything wrong with asking for something that so few have had?"

"I'm not a virgin, you know."

Donna smiled. She replaced the lid to the lunch box and placed it down on the coffee table. "No, I'm sure you're not." She reached down to the base of the bookcase next to her and withdrew a large sum of cash, placing it on top of the box. "Just in case you might think I don't have the agreed figure."

Alex looked around the place. "Yeah. Big danger of that." He glanced at the cash. "So how do you want to do this?"

CHAPTER 12

Alex followed her up to the second storey of the house. He carefully eyed the stairs leading to the next floor up. The house was narrow—as was the design at the time, but deep. The stairwell led up the left side of the house, the doors to the rooms on the right. High ceilings. Ornate décor ran around the fittings, lights, and such. There was a chandelier in one room. Donna walked into the first room on the right, holding the door open for him.

Alex wished he'd had the foresight to pick the cash up and pocket it before following her. He looked around the room quickly before crossing the threshold. It was a bedroom … of sorts. It certainly wasn't like anything he'd seen before.

The room was large, and square. In the centre of the wall was a bed—super king, at least. It was dressed in deep red—satin judging by the glisten in the light. The walls were dark—burgundy, probably. Alex shrugged at the thought. He wasn't an interior designer. Aside from that, the room was bereft of furniture. No wardrobes. Nothing. He stepped in. The carpet was lush, thick, and warm.

He noted a mirror on the ceiling above the bed.

Very tasteful.

Donna went to the oversized windows and drew the curtains almost to a close, before slinking across to Alex's side and turning the dimmer on, breathing a warm sensual light into the room. He nodded. "Very nice," he said quietly. She stood there next to him, breathing slowly. He could feel her warmth. "Where do you want me?" He smiled, turning to her. He assumed that she wanted him to be a dangerous man in the bedroom too. He couldn't help but feel a little silly, role playing as himself. Alex put his hand around the back of her neck and pulled her lips to his, kissing her hard. He felt her hand cup his balls. That, he wasn't expecting. He drew back and found her gently biting his lip. They stared into each other's eyes for a few seconds without words, before she released him.

"I want to fuck you," she whispered.

"Okay." Alex pulled his jacket off and dropped it to the floor behind him. He stuck his finger down the back of his tie and pulled it loose, but she put her hand on top of his, stopping him.

"Slow down," she said. Donna slid her fingers across the stubble he hadn't bothered to shave off today. He raised an eyebrow, if she wanted to be in charge, sure. Why not? She took Alex by the hand and led him to the edge of the bed. He let her. That was where she pulled his tie from him. She unbuttoned his shirt, slowly, all the while he watched her. She looked like she had undressed a man a thousand times. A pretty impressive feat for someone so young.

Unless she was a hooker, but that didn't make any sense.

She pulled his shirt over his shoulders and down, releasing him from it. He still resisted the urge to move. He wanted to grab her and throw her on the bed. He wanted to rip that fucking dress from her and fuck her hard. She unhooked his belt buckle. "Tell me how many men you've killed," she whispered.

Surprised, Alex muttered, "Uhh ..."

"Is it many?" Her fingers slipped into the front of his loosened trousers and found his cock, sliding it between them.

"Yes," he said, slightly too high pitched.

"Good," she said. Donna slipped her hands out and undid his trousers, pulling them down and releasing his cock. It strained inside his pants. "I see that you're excited."

"Yeah," he said. He reached to touch her and she brushed him away.

Her hand went inside his pants and she stroked him. He was fully erect now. If she was expecting some Don Juan performance out of him, she was going about it the wrong way. "Easy," he muttered. "That's dangerous. You don't want it going off."

She laughed. He hadn't meant for it to be a joke.

Donna yanked his pants down past his erection and then pushed him back onto the bed. He lay there, watching her. Fine. If she wanted to be in charge. "Up," she barked. She gestured to the top of the bed where Alex saw restraints for each of his hands. So it was like that, was it? He shuffled up the bed trying his best to be seductive, but probably failing miserably. Donna rolled her pencil dress up to her thighs, allowing her more free movement with her legs. Alex could see the clasps of her suspenders. Nothing higher.

Alex throbbed. He wanted in.

She straddled across him and took his left hand tying it tightly, giving it a hard pull to ensure the knot she used was inescapable. Then she did the same with his other hand. Alex just lay there. She was physically perfect, and he was living the dream. Why try to fight it? As soon as he was tied down, she got off him and stood next to the bed. She grinned at his cock. He was glad she liked it.

Then she turned and started out of the room.

"Uh, excuse me?" Alex said.

She turned and put her index finger to her lips. "One moment," she said, leaving the room.

Alex didn't like it. He looked at the knots on the ties. They were pretty solid knots. Maybe she'd been a sailor in a previous life. Urg. *Don't even think about that.* He looked at the bedpost he was tied to. That looked pretty weak, to be honest. There was some noise at the door and Donna returned. His cock responded by flexing. Nice to see the little fella was paying attention. She walked over to him and immediately took it in her hand, stroking him back to fully erect. Then she placed a small dish under the head of it. A Petri dish. "And ... that's for?" he asked.

"Just don't think about it," she said. She started to stroke him with a little more vigour, playing for an end game, rather than looking for some fun.

"What the fuck?" He was exasperated.

"Come on," she shouted. The door was pushed fully open and two more women came in. One of them was wearing leather. A long coat. More vampire hunter than mistress, Alex thought. The other was decked out in lacy shit.

"Look," he said. "There's plenty to go around, but …" he motioned with his head to his … head. "… you need to ease up on this, or it's all going to be over before it's started." The other two women busied themselves. One of them carried in a small folding table and the other something that looked like a pestle and mortar. They put it all together at the end of the bed and draped a red cloth over the table. "What the fuck is going on?"

"Are you going to cum for me?" Donna asked.

Alex looked at his cock. "Well, probably, yes." He answered honestly. He was struggling to see another outcome at this point.

"Good." She wanked him quicker.

"Oh, Jesus." He didn't know what was going on, but Alex felt that at this stage, giving them what they wanted was probably a bad idea.

"Is he nearly ready?" asked the one in leather.

"He is resisting, but yes," Donna replied.

"Good." Leather left the room again, leaving Lace standing there with a wooden box about the size of a ruler. Alex focussed on it. It was getting harder not to finish. She placed the box down and opened it, pulling out a blade. It was about a foot long, and curved. It looked antique and Turkish.

"What are you going to do with that?" he asked.

CHAPTER 13

Lace placed the knife down and smiled at Alex. "Don't worry. You have your own job to do." She came to the other side of the bed opposite Donna and poured herself onto the sheets. She ran her hands over his chest. "Why don't you let yourself go?" she whispered. "If you're really good, you can fuck us all later. Would you like that?"

Alex looked at her as she spoke. Yes. Yes he would like that. All three of the women were perfect. They were fucking Goddesses. And this all stank. *What was going on?* "Nah," he blurted.

"Oh please," she said, her voice turned to a whine. "Please let us fuck you. Over and over. We'll be good. I promise."

The begging did it.

Alex couldn't hold out any longer and streamed Alex juice into the dish. He grunted and flexed, and Donna stopped after a few strokes, getting out what she needed. He was *so* confused. Donna grinned at him. "See," she said. "Wasn't so hard, was it?"

"You should say that from here." Alex looked between the two women. He watched Donna take the dish and place it on the table at the end of the bed. "You want to give me a heads up now?"

Leather returned to the room. She was carrying a cage. She brought it to the end of the bed and placed it on the floor. Alex couldn't see, but he heard her open the cage and gently remove something. This was getting worse. It was going to be a snake, wasn't it? Alex watched her with trepidation as she stood, holding the cutest fucking white rabbit he'd ever seen. "Aww," he said. It looked at him with big red eyes, chewing on something.

Lace got up from the bed and went around to the table. She lifted a bowl onto it, and then joined Leather and the rabbit. She booped its nose. Donna got up from the bed and started to unzip her dress. "What … now?" Alex asked. "You could have done that a few minutes ago. It would have helped."

"Would it now?" she asked. Donna dropped the dress to her side, and Alex could see her for the first time. Underneath the dress she was naked apart from stockings and suspenders, her firm round breasts hung beautifully, and perky, and there was a mouth stretching from where her cunt should have been across her stomach and finished between the base of her tits. The mouth was on its side and after gaining sudden freedom it opened and closed, stretching. When it was open, Alex could see rows of teeth, malformed, broken, and between them squirmed a thousand unholy tongues, pushing globules of thick gelatinous drool around. "Does it make you hard, lover?" Donna asked.

"What the living fuck is that?" Alex screamed. "What are you?"

Donna smiled—with her human mouth. Well, the mouth on her face, anyway. She looked to Leather and Lace. "Ready?" she asked. Leather nodded, and Lace picked up the knife with a grin.

Leather was still holding the rabbit.

"No," Alex whispered. "Come on. What the fuck?"

Leather held the ears of the bunny in one hand and the feet of it with the other and stretched it out, while Lace took the dagger and stuck it into the creature at about the point its genitals would have been. Leather held the thing as it squirmed and fought against her grip, manoeuvring it over the bowl. Lace started a sawing action with the blade, pulling it up the belly of the creature, cutting it up like a steak. Alex had never heard the death screams of a rabbit before. He had always assumed that rabbits only made little mewling sounds like sleeping kittens. Maybe it was a hole in his knowledge base—of which he was running out of time to fill. He looked at the ties again, still unsure what the plan with him was.

And trying to ignore the not-human thing standing next to the bed.

As the blood squirted from the rabbit, its guts and bits of half-digested carrot spewed out into the bowl, the rabbit howled. It was the single most distressing thing that Alex had ever witnessed—a trophy held by the death throe of one particular woman in Norwich some years ago, but that was a different story—before today. Now, it was the Norwich woman, the rabbit screaming, and Donna, the not-human thing with the gaping mouth. Leather and Lace drained the rabbit as it squirmed its last, ensuring the deep thick juices flowed into the bowl. Then Leather discarded it to the table.

Donna watched the whole gruesome event while running her fingers sensually around the lips of the mouth in her stomach with one hand, while the other wandered gently over what may or may not have passed for a vagina. It was hard to tell from Alex's current perspective.

Alex wrapped the binds around his wrists and gripped them tightly in his fists.

Leather picked up the bowl, and her and Lace stepped back from the confines of the bed out into the space between the end of it and the wall. Donna went over to the two of them.

"What's going on?" Alex asked.

Donna waved over to him dismissively. "Don't worry. We'll get to you."

Fuck.

Lace stood, holding the bowl, and Leather dipped her hands into the warm liquid, making it overflow. The blood drooled over the top and leached down the side of the container. Donna gave a sharp intake of breath when it did, like she was getting some sexual satisfaction from seeing rabbit nectar flowing. Maybe she was? Leather withdrew her hands, reddened with the thick rabbit blood, bits of intestine and offal sticking to her flesh, and she started to paint the blood over the naked body of Donna. She dipped and painted across Donna's shoulders, masking her in gloop, working her way around methodically. Then she dipped into the blood again and cupped her hands, lifting some blood over to Donna, dribbling it over her breasts, as Donna shuddered.

Alex felt his cock twitch.

Jesus fucking Christ. Not now.

Donna notice and chuckled. "Well," she said as

Leather massaged the sticky red liquid into her beautiful, plump tits. "We are *dangerous*."

Alex looked down himself and he'd gone from dead-rabbit-flaccid, to half-mast. He smiled to himself and then shook his head back to the place it should be. Tied to the bed and almost guaranteed to die.

The unholy tongues were lapping out of the gash of a mouth, slurping at the vile liquid dribbling down Donna's flesh, lapping up the goodness, and as the lips reddened with blood, the mouth seemed to smile. Donna's flesh was glistening with some out-world like beauty as it rippled under the blood, and she held her head back now, flexing her whole body in orgasm.

Alex was hard at the sight, and didn't care. It was the most bizarrely erotic thing. Ever.

Donna screamed in pleasure, Alex looking around the room. Boner or not, he needed a get out clause in this contract. The mouth chuckled, obviously feeling the things Donna could. It sounded like Jabba the fucking Hutt cumming. Donna stumbled back, her legs weakening. Alex thought that given the chance he could have done that for her, without the other two women and the blood. And the rabbit. But never mind.

Leather and Lace placed the bowl down and stood subserviently at the end of the bed. Leather's hands were sticky with the blood of the small mammal. Lace's dress was splashed liberally with the blood. Ruined. That was never going to come out.

"He is happy," Donna said. "We are happy. Go.

Change," she ordered. The two women nodded in silence and left the room like military personnel.

"You have those two well trained," said Alex.

"I do. They are worthy of being my worshippers."

"About that …" Alex let the words drift into the room. "Any chance you could tell me what's going on?" He nodded at the mouth. "And, I don't know, what the fuck that is?" He tried to remain calm. Composed. Losing his shit wasn't going to get him out of this. Donna perched on the end of the bed. She was gently petting the corpse of the rabbit.

The mouth grunted contentedly. "There are worlds beyond this one, that you will never understand, Mr Cole. I know you said to call you Alex, but I think I might have outstayed the welcome on that one." She smiled, like it was a joke. "Worlds you will never witness. Even knowing what you know now, what you've seen today … once the ritual is complete, this world will be no more than a serving on a plate for a God you never worshipped, to consume."

"That all sounds like bullshit, love. But if I get your drift, you're ending the world? Yeah?" He glanced over to the petri dish that still sat on the table.

"Close enough, Mr Cole."

That was a turn up. Definitely not the way he thought today was going to go. Alex Cole: helping to end the world. Shit. He briefly considered what Chaisai wanted the Kuman Thong for, and thought that maybe he shouldn't be quite so easy—or cheap— with his complicity. For all he knew, that was two end of the world scenarios he might be actively participating in today alone. *Other worlds, huh? You learn something new every day.* "So what do you call this deity you have in, uh, your tummy hole?"

"You wouldn't be able to pronounce it without me inserting a reed from a clarinet into your vocal cords."

"Okay. Sounds like you've already tried that one. Never mind, eh?" He kept his eyes on her, using the opportunities he had to look around the room. His clothes had gotten kicked over to the wall near the door at some point. They were important—in the big scheme of things—but not a necessity. He looked at the petri dish. That was a different matter. He didn't really want to end the world today. He still had loose ends that needed resolutions.

Like the rest of his life.

CHAPTER 14

Donna stood and walked over to the window. She parted the curtains enough to be able to see out into the street.

"Just taking one last look?" Alex asked.

"Indeed," she replied.

"And what happens to you? I mean, *that* physical presence?"

"I will evolve." She still watched out the window.

Alex pulled the binds holding him tight, and raised his legs. He was trying to be silent. He wasn't as flexible in real life as he was in his mind. He expected to do this in one single, cool motion, but realised mid-manoeuvre that he didn't have the body strength of a young Van Damme. He struggled to pull his feet up over his face, but he managed to get them flat on the wall behind him, eventually. He ended with his arse proudly, nakedly, jutting into the air. Embarrassing? Possibly. Gaining leverage? Definitely. Alex pushed with his feet and pulled his arms, putting all the force on the bedposts that he was tied to.

There was a crack. It was loud enough to pull Donna from whatever thoughts she was having about ending the world or whatever, and she turned. Then the wood gave, freeing Alex from the bed. He flailed about like a beached whale for a second before getting his bearings, and getting upright.

Donna was charging across the room, her tits bouncing like a Benny Hill sketch, and her god-belly-mouth was open, tongues flapping.

Alex was plan-less. And without knowing what the plan was, he struggled to formulate something useful in the thirty nano-seconds he had before Donna was due to crash into him. Her god-maw was open wide enough to take a healthy chunk out of him. Naked him. He still had lumps of broken bedpost tied to his wrists. He flicked them around like nun chucks and landed each post in his hand like a stake. He brought them up like he was a god damned vampire hunter and thrust himself at Donna, wood first.

He spiked the two wooden stakes into the surprised Donna, one in her shoulder and the other into her side on the other side of the god mouth. Both missed the yawning monstrosity by a long way, and for that Alex was happy. She fell backwards, mostly under Alex's weight falling onto her, and the two of them ended on the carpet, Alex on top. The god mouth was between them, but Alex had managed to hold himself up out of the way.

They stared at each other for a second, Alex glad to be alive, and Donna possibly aghast. "You'll have to forgive my wood." Alex winked at her, and rolled off to the side. He sprang to his feet and made for his clothes.

Then he stopped.

He looked at the petri dish.

He still didn't know what they wanted it for—or him, come to that—, but he knew that he didn't want them to have it. He picked it up, as Donna got to her feet. The god mouth was crying out in frustrated confusion, and Donna screamed, "No!" Alex had to get rid of it. Before they got it back and attempted whatever it was they wanted to attempt with his love juice. But what? Where to get rid ... of ... it.

Aw, fuck. Alex sloshed the dish back, swigging his own spunk into his mouth. Donna screamed and lunged at him, but was too late, as she slammed into him, he discarded the dish to land in the corpse of the rabbit. He swirled the stuff around in his mouth as she tackled him to the ground.

The two of them pushed back and forth, and she managed to get on top, straddling him like she was going to cowgirl him, the god mouth chomping at him, trying to get a bite of something. Something Alex-y and squishy. Donna reached over to the table, picked up the sacrificial knife, and held it up like Van-fucking-Helsing.

Just swallow it. He didn't want to. It was still in his mouth, and if his mind had anything to say about it, that's where it was staying. *But it's yours*, his heart argued back. *No homo.* Alex closed his eyes and swallowed, thinking of England. "*Gaaahhh*, God."

Just as Donna stabbed the knife into his shoulder.

Lucky for Alex she was pretty shit at aiming, not so lucky was that the god mouth had given up waiting for her to deal with him, and it decided to start doing something itself.

As the two of them were so close, Donna still holding the knife, and her breasts lolling candidly on Alex's chest, the tongues of the god mouth squirmed out of the cavern in Donna's gut and started to probe around the edges of Alex's torso. They were trying to find purchase. Something to hold on to like they were attached to a desperate lover. Alex used his good hand to punch Donna on the side of the head, causing her to release the knife from her grip, but the tongues still wound their way around him.

The knife had gone through his shoulder, but Alex could immediately tell that it had missed all the important stuff, because he could still move his fingers. It wasn't the first time he'd been stabbed. With his good hand, he grabbed the hilt of the blade and yanked it from his body.

The pain ravaged him, causing his legs to coil, both at the same time. It was involuntary but they cracked Donna in the small of the back and caused her to arch herself back. A split second still of the scene would have showed two naked lovers, entwined together, a woman rolling back in the height of orgasm, her man, spent beneath her.

Quite far from the truth, in all told.

Blood was spitting up from the wound in Alex's shoulder, out, over his chest. Onto hers.

He swung the blade at the tongues of the god mouth and hacked at the slick flesh of them. Up close they clagged with gelatinous translucent glue, sticking the tentacle like appendages to anything they came close to. It was a cavalcade of grossness. The knife tore through them, and they squirted black god blood from the parts left attached to the god mouth. Alex rolled, getting Donna beneath him and pulled himself up onto his knees. She was screaming. The god mouth was screaming. The room was filled with a sound that Alex could barely comprehend. A cavern of white noise, shrieking a universe full of sound. *He* screamed, joining the choir of anger and pain. He pulled the knife up and stabbed it into Donna's tit, crashing through her perfect breast, into her torso. She stared wide eyed. Shock? Pain?

Black god blood spewed from the mouth.

Alex rolled off her, and onto the carpet. He got to his knees, and up. Blood ran free from the wound in his chest, he was slathered in god blood, and Donna writhed on the floor, noises emanating from her that were hitherto unheard in the annals of man.

The door opened and Leather and Lace returned. They were both wearing white robes. They looked like they'd joined a fucking convent in the time they'd been gone, but not a holy convent. Maybe a fetish one. Leather—or it could have been Lace, it was hard to tell now—was carrying a silver tray with a gold bowl on it, and Lace—the other one—was carrying a candelabra, ornate, with eight holders, a lit candle in each.

The two of them seemed surprised at the scene. Alex was impressed at how little sound must carry in a house this old. He charged across the room, wielding the knife towards Leather. She dropped the tray with the bowl on it at her feet and out spilled a thick, clear liquid. Over the carpet. Over her. She grabbed his arms, and the two of them fought for supremacy. She was strong. Stronger than Alex, he thought. He pushed her to the side and into Lace, who lost her balance, and dropped the candles.

They fell to the carpet and lit the liquid that had

been in the bowl. It was more flammable than petrol, the carpet lighting in an instant, turning the room into a lake of fire. Leather let him go, falling backwards as the flames tore up her legs, blistering her skin with tormenting speed.

Alex punched her with his bad hand as she fell away into the pool of flames. The pain from the stab wound sliced through him as he did, and he cursed himself for not just stabbing the bitch. Lace was on him. She clawed her finger nails down the side of his face, tearing his flesh off like it was no stronger than Christmas wrapping paper. Alex screamed and swung the blade at her, missing. He stumbled backwards, falling over Donna, who was now trying to get to her feet. The god tongues that he'd cut lolled in the mouth but others still licked out at him, trying to reach their prize.

Alex rolled over to the wall and found himself on his trousers. "Fucking hell," he blurted, grabbing one of the legs of them in a solid, if not painful fist. Donna ran at him and grabbed at him, missing and finding herself with the other leg of the trousers.

The two battled in a brief tug of war, one hand each on Alex's trouser legs. Then they gave, the arse ripping out of them, and them becoming two single legs. Alex rolled backwards onto the wall, and Donna fell into the flames, rolling in pain.

The room was hot. The temperature the liquid was burning at was furnace hot. It was like the four of them were trapped in a cremation oven. Alex felt the trousers. He had the pocket with the car keys.

That was something.

He looked across to the open door, out into the hallway, and pushed himself from the wall.

Then Lace came charging through the flames. Her white fetish habit was burning like the sun. The two of them collided, and fell back to the wall. Then she kneed Alex in the nuts. The sickness rose from them as they swelled, and Alex could think of nothing else to do, but head butt the cunt in the face. He slammed his forehead into her nose and she dropped backwards like a potato sack. "Fuck you," Alex whined through the pain. Her legs were on fire, and Alex was pissed.

He dropped across her and stabbed the knife into her gut, hoping she didn't also have a god mouth. The blade plunged into the soft sticky—human—flesh and Alex made a sawing motion, pushing with all his remaining strength across her gut. The red of her blood bloomed across the white of the habit and she screamed without fighting. Alex could feel the flames licking at his back, his skin scorching. He dropped the knife and punched his fist into the slit he'd created in the woman and grabbed whatever he could, yanking it out of her body and discarding it. He crawled from her prone corpse, frozen in death, with her guts plopped on top of her carved open belly.

He staggered to his feet and looked around the room, fires blazing across the carpet. The bed was on fire. His clothes, gone. He looked at the one trouser leg he held in his hand. Pain seared down his back from burns, his shoulder bled, his face throbbed.

"Fuck this," he said, looking over the wall of flames to the door beyond.

CHAPTER 15

Alex stamped out the flames from the sheets of the bed and then covered himself with them. He looked like a shit ghost. He ran at the wall of heat and through. The liquid—whatever it was—burned with a white magnesium light as the flames ripped upwards to the ceiling. It burned so hot the room was melting around him. It tore the skin from his feet as he passed through it.

"Fuck, fuck, fuck," he yelped as he careened through. He burst onto the landing, coughing his guts up as smoke descended from the ceiling. The house was filling with it. He ran naked down the stairs, still holding onto his trouser leg. He fumbled through the pocket, and pulled the car keys out.

While he always attempted to maintain at least an illusion of anonymity, an air of mystique, he felt like maybe he'd missed the mark on this job. He reached the bottom of the stairs and stalled. He felt like he was missing something.

"Oh fuck," he uttered. He turned the cornered of the bannister and headed to the room at the end of the hallway.

The haunting cry of the god mouth came from upstairs. Alex didn't know if it was a death cry, or if the thing was actually fine, and just really, really, pissed at him. Judging by the day he'd had, probably the latter. Alex ran into the room and grabbed the lunch box and the cash off the coffee table.

Waste not, want not.

He then ran for the front door.

———

He yanked the front door open, lunch box and cash in one hand, car keys in the other, trouser leg draped over his arm. He'd had enough of today, and was about ready for a drink. He stared out of the burning house to the crowd that was forming on the street, looking up as the glass from the floor above was shattering, smoke billowing out into the air.

Naked, burned, and bleeding, Alex could only think of one thing to do. Faced with the elite of Knightsbridge, he quickly took the trouser leg and wrapped it around the lunch box.

He started running.

"Everybody move. *I've got a burned baby here.* There's no time. I need to get to the hospital." Statements of which, mostly were true. The rich, richer, and royal parted like the Red Sea for the naked hero running from a burning building to save a child.

Suckers.

Alex left a trail of blood on the pavement as it let from the burns on his feet. He ran to the corner and around. The fuckers were actually applauding him. Around the side of the park, he pressed the fob, and unlocked the car. He opened the door and chucked the lunch box into the foot well, and got in, starting the engine. He popped the glove box and pulled out his phone, swapping it for the cash.

Pulling away, he followed the one-way system for a minute, driving at break-neck speeds, mostly for the sakes of the onlookers, but once he was nearer The Thames he dropped to a reasonable pace, and sunk down as far into the seat as he could, so that people couldn't see he was shirtless in the car.

He drove for the edge of the City.

No time to play.

He dialled Jax.

"Afternoon," she said. He could *hear* her smile. "I haven't left you any messages. What's up?"

"Job from Donna what's her face—done, fee paid in full. I'll drop your commission to the usual account tonight."

"Cool," she said. "I take it a good time was had by all. I don't know how you do it."

"Yeah," he said, wincing as his foot stuck to the clutch, leaving behind some skin. "I blew my load. Set her whole body on fire. I think I saved the world too."

"With your penis. Yeah."

Alex let the snark in her voice go. "It's all good. But look, if she calls back, no offense, but she was bit weird. Find out what she wants, get her number, but don't agree to anything. This boat's sailed."

"No problem. Mrs Philips is a wacko." Alex could hear her scribbling down a note. "How are you getting on with Human Song?"

"*Kuman Thong.*" He glanced at the box sliding about on the floor of the car. "Fine. One down. I should be finished in a couple of days. Can you find out where I can buy something to coat the little fuckers in gold?"

CHAPTER 16

Charming his way into someone's guts wasn't going to work with three deep *cat* scratches down his face. He looked like he'd tried to rape someone in an alleyway and they'd fought back. Having a massive bandage to cover it wasn't exactly appealing either.

So he had to try a change in tact.

Alex stood in full scrubs in Queens Hospital—the largest hospital in a twenty mile radius outside of Ashbury. He didn't want to risk the local one for obvious reasons. It was late evening. The perfect time for him to nose around with little chance of being challenged by anyone. The staff were few and far between and visiting hours were long finished. He was looking at the map of the building. He'd arrived at maternity, but discovered it was a hive of activity.

Obviously it would be, what with it being full of screaming little fuckers.

He left and was now trying to work out what might be the next best thing, when his eyes fell on a different department. It was thin, but there was a possibility that he could shop there. Worth a try—what did he have to lose apart from a few minutes?

He swung his backpack on his back and followed the directions the map gave in the direction of the morgue.

The hospital was completely bereft of security. Alex assumed there must be some there somewhere, but there weren't any actively guarding anything.

Good. He turned the corridor under the sign for the Mortuary. The happy, cheery signs that had adorned every wall he'd walked passed so far became further between, until they disappeared, and somehow a deep sadness enveloped everything as he walked. *Shit, they should make this place less depressing.* As he reached the double doors to the morgue, the silence was overpowering.

The whole corridor was soul sucking.

Jesus.

He pushed his way through the doors into the corridor beyond. The lights were out in this one. He'd taken one step beyond the public walkway. Alex looked back through the door. There was no one back there. He'd seen barely a soul in the last five minutes. Letting the door go, he flipped the lights on in the corridor. There was an open waiting area to the right and a closed off one to the left. After that there was an office, and beyond that the closed sterile door to the mortuary.

Alex hurried over to it and pushed against it. It was locked, as he expected it would be. He swung his backpack from his shoulder and got his lock pick kit out from inside. He'd picked it up on Amazon, and with the help of a few Youtube tutorials, had become pretty adept at hacking his way through most things. It was amazing the shit you could buy on the Internet to almost exclusively help you be a criminal. He poked around in the lock with the picks. He'd been doing this sort of shit for some time now, and it never really got easy. Just *easier*.

Finally a satisfying click rattled through the

darkness and Alex opened the door, sliding into the black beyond. He looked around cautiously before turning the lights on. There were no windows in here—not even in the doors to the corridor.

And it was cold.

He flipped the light switch by the door and the buzz and rattle of shitty fluorescent lighting filled the silence before the room was bathed in a cold blue light. It was all very welcoming.

Alex half expected there to be tables with bodies covered by sheets lining the room, but maybe that was just in the movies? There were tables, but they were disappointingly empty. He went to the far wall. Lots of miniature little doors in rows. That was more like it. Alex opened the first. Pair of feet. Slightly blue. "Voila," he announced in a whisper.

He pulled the drawer out with the body on it. There was a sheet over the corpse, and Alex could tell immediately that it was a man, so no use at all. But his morbid curiosity got the better of him, and he pulled the sheet back. There were few defining features on the corpse except a penis. The gentleman's head was caved in, as was his chest. He'd been cleaned up well, so there was no blood and bits of inside on him, but Alex assumed that due to the trauma, there could be very little in the way of insides, *inside*, either. He read the tag on the guy's foot. "Well, Carson." *RTA*, it read. He let the tag drop and picked up the sheet to recover him. He glanced at his massive cock. "Lucky boy," he said, re-covering him with the sheet and pushing the drawer back into the freezer. He closed the door. Moved to the next one.

The first four were men. Clearly the town had a vendetta against men. The fifth was a woman.

Alex looked at the tag. This was taking far longer than he'd hoped it would, but if he'd stopped reading all the tags, he'd be moving quicker. This woman had died of … self-inflicted asphyxiation. He looked up her body, and imagined that she was stunning when she wasn't so stiff. He walked up her and let his fingers slide across her cold skin, along the scars left by the autopsy. "Shame," he whispered. "You shouldn't let the bastards win." He covered her back up and moved on to the next one.

Another woman. This time, she was either chubs, or pregnant. He pulled the sheet back. Looking at her, she looked pregnant. She was showing—or possibly bloated from the gasses that turn up after death. Alex had heard that you can shit yourself even hours after. He pushed on her belly and listened. No farting sounds. That was a good sign. She also had no scarring across her stomach, so if there was a little fucker in there, it was still there. He had no idea how old the kid was, though.

Alex looked around the room and quickly found a set of tools. He couldn't tell if they were sterilized or not. He glanced at the woman. But who cared, right? He dragged the tray of tools over, expecting to use nothing but the scalpel. "Okay," he whispered to the woman. "This is gonna hurt you, more than me." He raised his finger without continuing, and then checked the tag. He grinned. "Margaret Philips." He looked her in the face. "Your namesake fucked up my shoulder, you know." He took the scalpel and pushed it with ease into the top of the woman's stomach, drawing it down towards her pubic mound, keeping the blade from slipping into the flesh too much. He still didn't have much of a grasp on the intricacies of where baby bodies were laying inside the mummy body.

The skin felt different to cut through, compared to the last one. It felt more rubbery. Less tactile. He finished the cut—impressed with the knife—and placed it back on the tray. Pushing the two sides of the woman apart, he saw a child inside. Perfect. He reached in and cupped the kid corpse. It was like rummaging around in the fridge in the supermarket trying to find the best joint of pork. There were no fluids inside her like the last one. Alex guessed that she'd dried out to a husk. He didn't know how long she's been dead for, but maybe it had been a few days.

Maybe she was leaking?

He pulled the dead foetus from the womb and held it up like a prized fish. It looked about the same size as the other one, which was probably a good sign. He placed it carefully on the cut open corpse.

Alex retrieved the lunch box from his back pack. He brought it up and took the lid off, using it as a measure of the size of the kid.

Perfect.

He put the kid in the lunch box and packed it with the towels he'd brought. He'd cook it later. Then he packed everything away into the backpack and slung it over his shoulder. He looked at Margaret. "Sorry about all this," he said, waving over her defiled corpse. "Bills to pay, you understand?" He covered her back up and pushed her back into the cabinet. That was sure going to be a surprise for someone in a couple of days. He turned to leave and then stopped at the tray of tools. He hummed for a couple of seconds and then picked up the leather scalpel storage pouch. He made sure it was full and took it with him.

Looking out the door, Alex made sure the corridor into the Mortuary was still empty, and he left, not bothering to lock the door behind him. He returned to the next doors and flipped the corridor lights off.

He peered through the door into the hospital beyond. There was a woman crying in one of the seats that lined the walls. Damn. Alex watched her. He wasn't really keen on being seen leaving the morgue.

He waited.

And waited.

She was still sitting there weeping. Fucking hell. He looked around the corridor, and went over to the reception desk. Behind it was a pack of disposable masks. *At last, a stroke of luck.* He pulled one over his face and strode with confidence from the morgue.

In the corridor he went to pass the woman—and ignore her—when she looked up and said, "Doctor, do you have a minute?"

Alex wanted to ignore her. He *wanted* to tell her to go fuck herself, and that he had far more pressing matters to deal with. He slid his fingers over the leather scalpel case in his hand. He stopped and politely asked, "What is it?" It was the only way he could think of to not draw attention to himself. He stood over her, intimidation drew powerful emotions. But she patted the seat next to her. Alex sighed, but perched next to her anyway. "What is it?" he asked, again with a little more sympathy.

"I've been diagnosed with cancer," she said. "It's terminal."

That was terrible, yes. But Alex really didn't have time for it. "Have you seen a councillor?"

She nodded, "Of course, yes. But ..."

But...? "Go on."

"I've only been given six months, and I just found out I'm four months pregnant. I don't know what to do."

Alex sat back. "Maybe I can help." He rested the leather pouch on his knee.

Epilogue

Alex hurried out of the front door of the hospital with one long dead foetus in a lunch box in his backpack and a fresh one in a steel kidney dish, with another steel kidney dish on top of it like a shit takeaway. Still it was warmer than the last pizza he had delivered. He had fresh blood down his scrubs, but he didn't want to hang around and change. It was going to be light soon, and while he wasn't worried about his work in the morgue earlier in the night, the impromptu too-late abortion he did—with surgical precision—in the makeshift operating room—the ladies toilets—might raise some angst among the other patrons.

Especially finding the corpse of a cancer patient cut up in the stall.

He opened the car boot and slung the backpack, leather pouch full of scalpels—he was keeping them—and kidney dishes in, covered it all with a rug and slammed the boot. He got in, and flipped the lights on, heading out of the car park, and driving hard for the main road back to Ashbury.

Alex pulled the tray from the oven, and poked the two foetuses. The one from the dead woman hadn't gotten a good crackling on it like the fresh one. He shrugged. While it didn't matter, it really was a case of live and learn. He rested the tray on the top of his oven, the smell of roasting meat wafting out into the room.

He sat at the table and looked at the third one—the one he'd gotten out of the fridge earlier. Jax had sent him *gold leaf* to coat the little fuckers with. It was a weird fucking thing. Actual gold—cost a goddamn fortune—but wafer thin. It was even edible. Apparently chef's used it. Where? He didn't know. The local kebab shop sure as shit didn't use gold fucking leaf in their dishes. Might have used dead babies by the quality of the food sometimes, though. He shook his head looking at the attempt he'd made in gold leafing the little guy.

It was covered, sure, but it looked shit.

His gaze moved over to the two cooling on the side. They were going to be easier. He'd given up on the gold leaf now and had a new idea.

As they cooled, Alex moved them onto a cake rack. At least this job had managed to up his bakeware collection. Once he'd cleared this stuff out of his kitchen, he really should try his hand at actually making a cake.

Maybe use some fucking gold leaf.

Alex picked up the can of gold car spray paint he'd picked up from the local pound shop and shook it, irritated. Why was this taking so long?

Patience, he thought to himself. He picked up his phone and dialled Chaisai. "Mr Cole," he answered.

"Hi. I've finished with the job. I have the collectibles you asked me to source. I take it that the payment is in place?"

"I have your money, Mr Cole."

"Good. Look. I had a job go hard left on me

recently, and I ended up … let's just say that there was some mystic shit going on, possibly interdimensional beings, and, well, the end of the world was mentioned more than once."

"What has this got to do with me, Mr Cole?"

"You don't even sound surprised."

"There are many things in this world that you don't understand. There are many things that most people do not, and will never discover about what is going on in the world. Threats of the end of the world happen daily, I'm sure. They do not surprise me."

"Huh." Alex thought for a second, before continuing. "You said that these collectibles were required for the black arts."

"I did."

"I just want to make sure that they aren't going to be used to, let's say, end the world, or anything."

"They will not. Their usage will have no bearing on you after the delivery."

"Good. I'll get Jax to call you later with the details on the drop."

"As you wish, Mr Cole." The call dropped. Alex nodded into the phone, giving the kids a quick prod to test their temperature. They were about ready for spraying.

He dialled Jax. "Hey," she answered.

"I'm about ready for the drop for Chaisai. Secure. Somewhere in Kent. I'm too tired to travel."

"Cool."

"Oh, and when you next update whatever advertisements you're using for me at the moment, can you add something to the end?"

"Of course. What?"

"Paranormal and interdimensional work accepted. Deities slain. Reasonable rates."

About the Author

Ash is a British horror author. He resides in the south, in the Garden of England. He writes horror that is sometimes fantastical, sometimes grounded, but always deeply graphic, and black with humour.

www.ashericmore.com

Made in United States
North Haven, CT
03 July 2024